Snowbaby Could Not Sleep

by Kara LaReau

Illustrated by
Jim Ishikawa

Megan Tingley Books
LITT COMPANY
New York Boston

Little, Brown and Company
Time Warner Book Group
1271 Avenue of the Americas, New York, NY 10020
Visit our Web site at www.lb-kids.com

First Edition: October 2005

Library of Congress Cataloging-in-Publication Data

LaReau, Kara.
Snowbaby could not sleep / by Kara LaReau ; illustrated by Jim Ishikawa.—1st ed.
p. cm.
Summary: Unable to get Snowbaby to fall asleep on a snowy winter night, Snowpapa and Snowmama decide that a more creative solution than counting snowflakes is needed.
ISBN 0-316-60703-7
[1. Bedtime—Fiction. 2. Snowmen—Fiction.] I. Ishikawa, Jim, ill. II. Title.
PZ7.L32078Sn 2004
[E]—dc22

2004003644

10 9 8 7 6 5 4 3 2 1

Book design by Tracy Shaw

TWP

Printed in Singapore

The illustrations for this book were done in mix medium,
gouache, watercolor, and oil pastel.
The text was set in Humana Sans, and the display type is Aitos.

To my mother, Patricia LaReau
—K.L.

For my parents and my brother, Hideto
—J.I.

It was a snowy, windy, cozy winter night,
and everyone had gone to bed.

But Snowbaby could not, would not sleep.
"I can't sleep," he said to Snowpapa.
"I'm not tired yet."

"Try counting snowflakes," said Snowpapa.
So he did.

But Snowbaby could not, would not sleep.
"I can't sleep," he said to Snowmama.
"I'm too hot."

Snowmama put an extra blanket of snow on his bed.

But Snowbaby could not, would not sleep.
"I can't sleep," he said to Snowpapa.
"Will you sing to me?"

Snowpapa sang "Winter Wonderland."
Then he sang "Frosty the Snowman."
Then he sang "Let It Snow, Let It Snow, Let It Snow."

But Snowbaby could not, would not sleep.
"I can't sleep," he said to Snowmama.
"I'm thirsty."

Snowmama poured him a cold glass of water…
with extra ice.

But Snowbaby could not, would not sleep.
"I can't sleep," he said to Snowpapa.
"The wind is too loud."

Snowpapa gave Snowbaby his earmuffs.

But Snowbaby could not, would not sleep.
"I can't sleep!" he cried.
"I'm lonely! Stay with me and keep me company!"

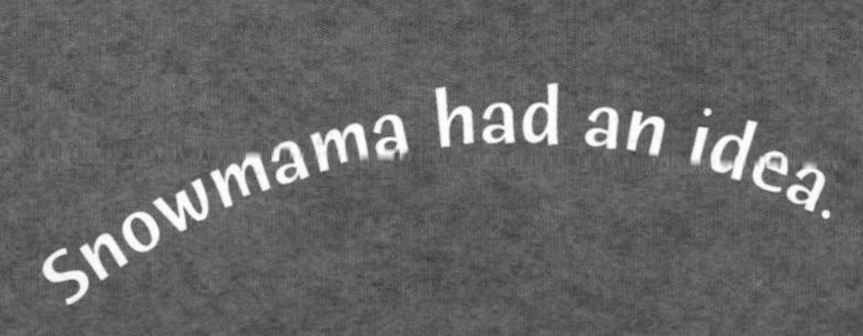

Snowmama had an idea.

She scooped up the softest, whitest snow.
She packed it together tightly.

Then, Snowmama and Snowpapa went to work.

Snowpapa snipped two buttons from his vest.
Snowmama clipped a bit of ribbon from her skirt.

Together, they made Snowbaby a very special surprise.

"A Snowdoggie!" said Snowbaby.

"It has my eyes," pointed out Snowpapa.
"And Snowmama's smile."

"It will keep you company," said Snowmama.

Snowbaby curled up under the blankets
with Snowdoggie.

All was quiet and still.

But Snowdoggie could not, would not sleep.

"What's the matter, Snowdoggie?

Are you too hot?

Are you thirsty?"

"Is the wind too loud?

Do you need someone to sing to you or keep you company?"

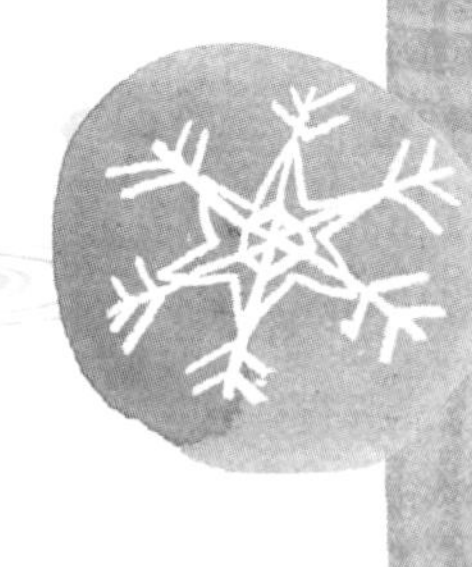

"It's okay. I'm here," Snowbaby said, patting Snowdoggie on his frosty head and drawing him close.

“Let’s count snowflakes until we fall asleep,” Snowbaby said.
So they did.

"Goodnight, Snowbaby," whispered Snowmama.

"Sleet dreams, Snowdoggie," whispered Snowpapa.

Then Snowmama and Snowpapa tiptoed to their own bed.

And finally, everyone could, would, and did drift to sleep,

snuggled under their blankets of snow.

Good night!
Sleet dreams!